THE REFLECTION IN ME

by MARC COLAGIOVANNI Art by PETER H. REYNOLDS

A Scholastic Australia book

"I like being you,"

said the reflection in the mirror.

"To me, you are perfectly perfect."

I blushed. "Me?"

"Yes, you! And by the way, you have wonderful eyes."

I blinked, astonished. "I do?"

"Absolutely!

They sparkle like stars on the darkest of nights."

I gazed downwards. "Thank you.

Your eyes sparkle, too."

"Sweet of you to say!

You have a marvellous voice."

I gently whispered, "You really think so?"

"Of course!

You sound as joyous as a songbird whistling in the trees.

And you have a magnificent smile."

I sheepishly grinned.

"Well . . . Momma always says, 'Start every day with a smile.'"

"I agree!

Your smile is as bright and cheerful as the sun in the sky."

"And you are quite smart."

I took a step towards the mirror.

"I do try very hard."

"You sure do.

You are as brilliant as a rocket scientist!"

"I like that you are friendly."

I leaned in closer.

"It's very important to be caring, you know."

"It sure is. You're as gentle as a butterfly."

"And you have a lot of courage."

I raised my head high.

"I auditioned for the school play today!"

"Outstanding! You're as brave as a lion!"

"You're a lovely dancer."

I spread my arms wide. "Watch how fast I can twirl!"

Around and around I went.

"Amazing! You're as graceful as a dolphin gliding through the sea."

I plopped on the floor giggling
as the room playfully spun around me.

"And you have a terrific laugh!"

"Thank you very much!"

"Your chuckle fills the air with bubbly joy."

"But most of all . . . I like your heart.
Your kindness is as beautiful as a rainbow."

I stood up and
walked towards the mirror.
"To me, you are perfectly perfect."
I gently pressed
my hands against the glass.

"I like being you,"
said the reflection in the mirror.
We smiled in unison.
"I like being you, too.
I want to be you forever."

May you
always see yourself
as you truly are...
perfectly perfect.
—MARC COLAGIOVANNI